D0786263

Krupinski, Loretta.
The royal mice : the
sword and the horn /
c2004.
33305208865430
ca   06/24/05

THE ROYAL MICE

THE SWORD AND THE HORN

Loretta Krupinski

Hyperion Books for Children

New York

SANTA CLARA COUNTY LIBRARY

. 3 3305 20886 5430

copyright © 2004 by Loretta Krupinski
All rights reserved. No part of this book may be reproduced or transmitted
in any form or by any means, electronic or mechanical, including photocopying, recording, or by any
information storage and retrieval system, without written permission from the
publisher. For information address Hyperion Books for children,
114 Fifth Avenue, New York, New York 10011-5690.

First Edition
1 3 5 7 9 10 8 6 4 2
Printed in Singapore
Reinforced binding
Library of congress cataloging-in-publication Data on file.
ISBN 0-7868-1836-0 (tr.)
visit www. hyperionbooksforchildren.com

GUINEVERE

CADBURY

LITTLE FRANCIS

GILBERT
the ELDER

THE QUEEN of All You Can See lived in a castle high. She had servants, rubies galore, and everything nice, but to her dismay, she also had mice.

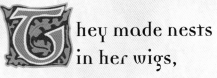
They made nests in her wigs,

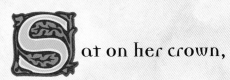
Sat on her crown,

lept inside her shoes,

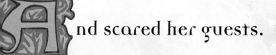nd scared her guests.

The queen called out to her servants. "No more mice! Bring me the biggest cat in the kingdom," she said in a voice not so nice.

Some cats were too small, too shy, too old, too fat. And then there was Max the Magnificent. His claws glistened in the light. His tail stood straight up and twitched like a whip.

The queen received him on her throne. "I am hopeful that you can rid my castle of mice. Search anywhere you wish."

Max bowed before the queen and replied, "*If there be mice in here, then may they shake with fear. Hide they may, but Max the Magnificent is my name and Seek is my game.*" And then he hissed, "*S-s-s-s-s-s-s-s-s.*"

He hoped to make the queen very proud.

ax swaggered and slunk into each chamber and every dark corner of the castle. His magnificent tail twitched; his whiskers wiggled up and down.

A–A–A–H, the scent of mice was everywhere. It was so delicious, he could hardly stand it. "S-s-s-s-s-s."

nd soon the scent of cat was everywhere, too. The royal mice couldn't stand that, either. Cadbury and Guinevere peeked out at Max, asleep on the queen's bed.

"Huh—he must be tired from hunting our friends all night," said Cadbury.

Guinevere was alarmed. "I'm scared," she said.

"Me too," said Cadbury.

"What can we do? None of us is safe anymore. I don't want to lose you," said Guinevere. And a small tear, the size of the head of a pin, fell from her eye, oh my.

Cadbury reached for her paw and said, "We must hide in tiny, secret places and learn to disguise ourselves. Come, I will show you how."

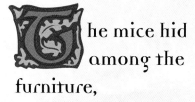he mice hid among the furniture,

gainst the palace wall,

n the kitchen,

And in the queen's bedroom, where Guinevere gathered the hair that fell from the royal hairbrush and used it to soften her bed.

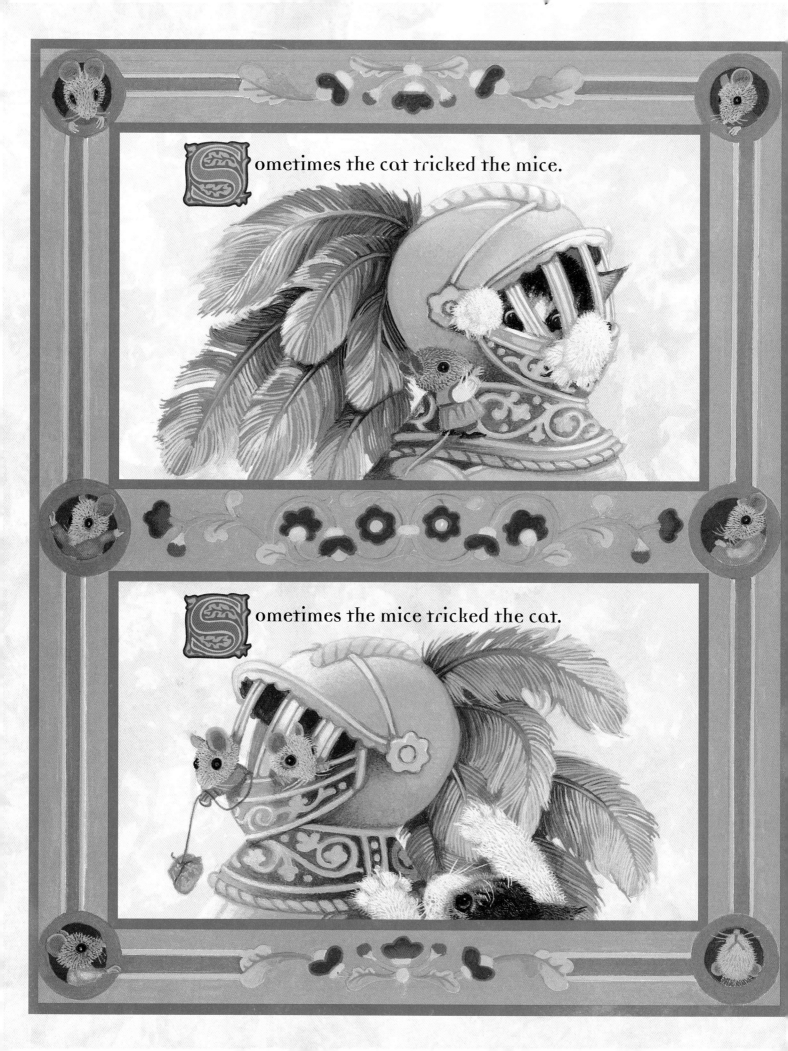

Sometimes the cat tricked the mice.

Sometimes the mice tricked the cat.

As good as the mice were at hiding, it wasn't good enough. Max was finding them.

Cadbury and Guinevere summoned all the mice to a meeting behind a bookcase. The glow from their candles could not be seen from behind so many books.

"The life we once knew has changed," said Cadbury. "I know we are hiding as best we can, but sadly, some of us have lost friends and family. We must find a way to chase the cat from the castle."

Gilbert the Elder stood up. "I believe I can help us. There is a legend that was handed down to me from my grandfather, who heard it from his father, who heard it from his father, who—"

Guinevere interrupted him, much to the relief of the other mice, and said, "Please go on with the story, dear."

"There is a secret chamber somewhere in the castle," Gilbert continued. "Inside are a sword and a horn. When the sword is grasped and the horn is blown, spirits will rise up. They are the spirits of the mice who were once brave warriors, and who lived here long ago. It is said that they will help whoever grasps the sword and blows the horn."

In a reverent tone, Cadbury said, "If this be true, then we can rid the castle of the cat. Let's go find the chamber."

Once again, but with hope in their hearts, the mice hid from the watchful eyes of Max. They explored up and down, in and out, over every inch of the castle, looking for the hidden chamber.

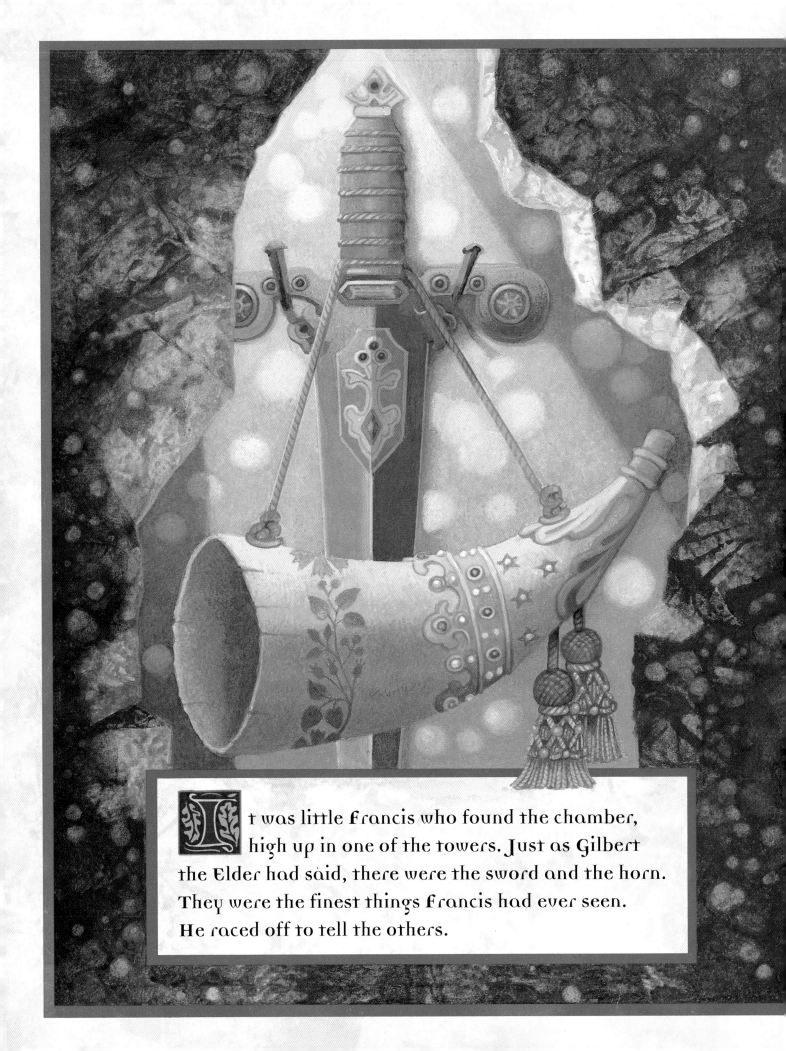

It was little Francis who found the chamber, high up in one of the towers. Just as Gilbert the Elder had said, there were the sword and the horn. They were the finest things Francis had ever seen. He raced off to tell the others.

veryone gathered in the hidden chamber.
Cadbury trembled, for he had never seen
spirits, and he was afraid; but he knew what he
must do.

With a sigh bigger than he was himself, Cadbury
grasped the sword. So that Max wouldn't hear it, he
blew the horn as quietly as he could.

Suddenly, the chamber filled with the glow of hundreds of pairs of red eyes—the spirits of the long-ago mice.

Cadbury stepped up to the nearest spirit. "A cat now lives in the castle and is trying to get rid of us," he said. "Can you help us?"

A voice rose from amid the gathering of spirits. *"We may be small and not very tall, but we will fight and never fall."*

Everyone in the chamber rejoiced—quietly.

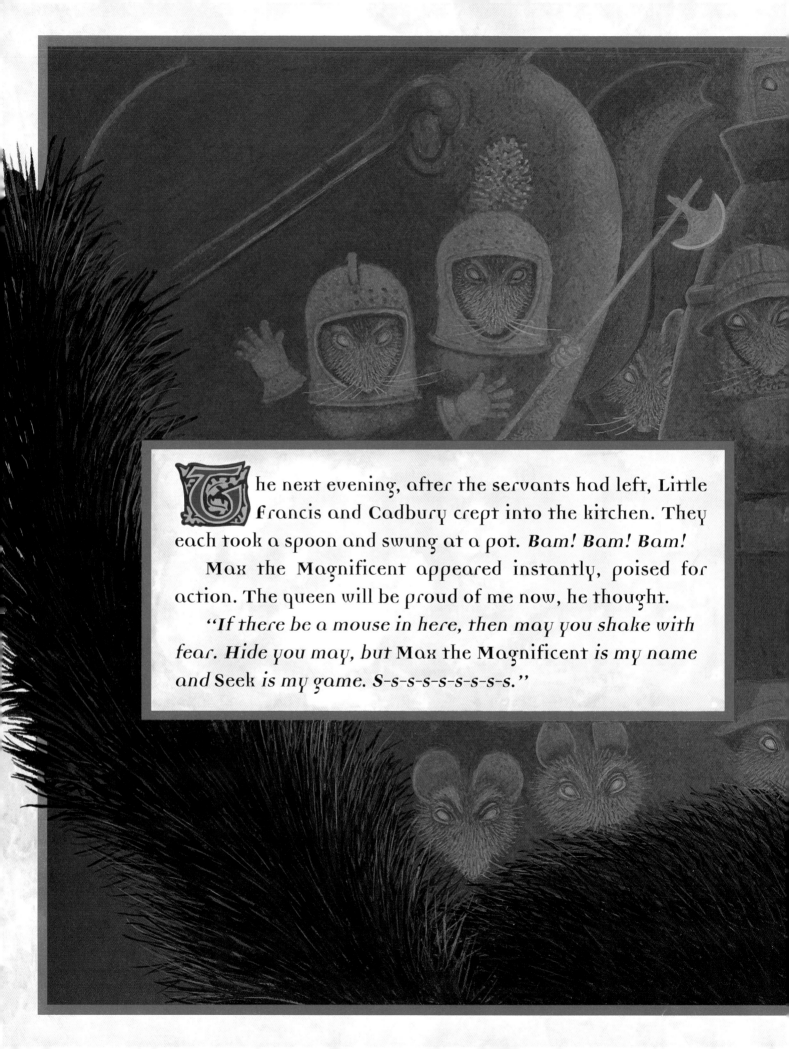

The next evening, after the servants had left, Little Francis and Cadbury crept into the kitchen. They each took a spoon and swung at a pot. *Bam! Bam! Bam!*

Max the Magnificent appeared instantly, poised for action. The queen will be proud of me now, he thought.

"If there be a mouse in here, then may you shake with fear. Hide you may, but Max the Magnificent *is my name and* Seek *is my game. S-s-s-s-s-s-s-s-s."*

is tail twitched; his whiskers wiggled. The scent of mouse was everywhere. But much to his surprise, instead of mice, he saw only hundreds of pairs of red eyes piercing the darkness.

He hissed and he pounced. Those beady red eyes were everywhere. He chased them into the sink, into the kettle, up on a shelf, and over the table, before landing upside down in the woodbox. His sharp claws glistened in the twilight, but all they could grasp was the thin, cold air that always comes with spirits.

"What good is a cat if he can't catch mice?" said the queen, peering around the doorway.

Max, suddenly not so magnificent anymore, was scared. He could smell the mice, but he could not see them. This place is haunted, he thought.

Max said to his mistress, *"If there be mice in here, then they can stay, it's clear. I've done my best, Queenie. The mice have won, though they be teeny."*

Still trying to look magnificent, Max scrambled out of the castle, letting out a loud hiss as he fled. He was never seen again.

Cadbury replaced the jeweled sword and the horn in the tower for another time, another battle.

he **Queen of All You Can See** could never keep another cat in the castle. Her Royal Highness learned to live with the royal mice, and they learned to live with her.

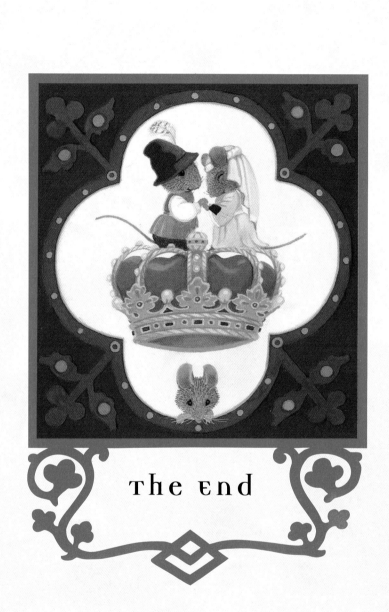

the end